The Goddess

"Who will take me to meet the Goddess?" I was in a tiny, open-air bar and I was talking out loud, deliberately. All the tourist boats had turned me down or had feigned ignorance or had actually been ignorant. It seems that up and down the river those that knew of the Goddess wanted nothing to do with the Goddess. I posed the question to the bartender who shrugged his shoulders at me, but I was addressing everyone. This seedy little bar was where the local merchant boat captains came to drink, apparently. I was half way up the murky Amazon. A large ferry had brought me to Manaus the largest "city" in the middle of the Amazon river. Going further up river would require a smaller boat and someone who knew of the final location of "the Goddess". These captains, if that's indeed who they were, looked at each other, muttered something in Portuguese and laughed. It was funny of course, I was assuming that everyone spoke English. A fairly silly idea but tourists were still plentiful this far up river. I had listened to the sounds of the Amazon on the way in. The ferry had been huge with room for cars and lots of fresh produce. The passengers laid in hammocks on the upper deck (very civilised). I'd seen almost nothing of the local wildlife that the Amazon is famous for, only Amazon river dolphins and one giant otter, but I'd been assured that all that was about to change. If the canopy of bird calls, monkey screeches and the occasional growl that had greeted me between the tiny fishing villages was anything to go by I wasn't sure I wanted to meet the local wild life. This was lion and tigers and bears country (figuratively speaking).

My name is Marc Durwood and I'm tracking down the mysterious "Goddess" to escape the mysterious secret society that is "The Sisterhood,". How did I end up 4500 miles south of my humble life in the States? Well that is a *long* story. I'm just a lecturer of particle physics at Straightwoods university and I want to return to my job. Three of my students Amanda, Rachelle and Iris pulled me into their powerful sex cult. Well let's be fair, they seduced me. And they had some powerful means of persuasion. Since then I've met more members of the Sisterhood than I can remember and loved them all. My travels have taken me through Paris to Borneo and now finally deep into the Amazon river where I'm assured that the Goddess lives – off grid - in her own compound. But my leads were running dry. Wherever I went people assured me that there was no Goddess or feigned ignorance or just bluntly refused. I'd been in Manaus 2 days and in Brazil for more than 2 weeks and now. Just as it seemed that I was getting close the trail was running dry.

"I'd pay cash," I pressed the Barman, "American 200 dollars," I looked around the room, nothing except laughter.

"Do not take it personally Mr Durwood," the Barman chuckled in broken English. It wasn't the first time I'd tried in this bar, "They are afraid,"

"Oh I know. I mean this is the mighty Amazon in the tough country of Brazil!" I raised my voice, "But up and down the river it's the same. People are afraid of one tiny woman!"

"Mr Durwood," hissed the Barman as he pressed a shot glass of fourth grade whiskey into my hands.

An old, white haired and whiskered gentleman got up, slowly came over and sat beside me, "Francii, here," and he paid the Barman, "So we are cowards are we?"

"It just seems that there isn't enough money to stop people from pissing their pants and going up that river!" I shot my glass – I was getting used to pretending I was in the wild west. Well it was the wild south.

"Maybe it is the company you keep,"

"I'm alone,"

"Really? So why do you want to meet this Goddess?"

"I want the freedom to go home,"

"You are free now Mr? Oh my name is Zarek?"

"Durwood, Marc Durwood," as in Bond, James Bond - this is fun. It was a firm handshake, "and you may think I'm free, but I assure you it's an illusion,"

"I wouldn't be too sure which one of us is living in an illusion Mr Durwood. So freedom lies with the Goddess yes?"

"Yes … hopefully,"

Zarek said something to Francii in Portuguese who smiled and left us.

"Do you know what we call the Goddess here in the Amazon Mr Durwood?"

"Marc please,"

"Moura Encantada,"

"That's pretty what does that mean?"

"The Enchanted Woman. Legend tells of a beautiful woman who transforms into a terrifying snake. She guards an enormous treasure. It is said that anyone who breaks her spell will have the gold and marry virgins,"

"Gold would be nice. Virgins I can do without,"

"Still she doesn't frighten you?"

"Well yes … but I need to go,"

"Well if your hard on is so big for the Goddess I will take you, but it will cost you Mr Durwood,"

"200 US dollars,"

"3,"

"3!"

"Where else do you have to go Mr Durwood?"

"When do we leave?"

"Meet me at the dock at sunset. You can't miss me, I have the smallest boat on the Amazon,"

"Sunset then, thank you Zarek," we shook hands, "Good to see not everyone is a coward,"

"Oh I am afraid Marc. As you should be," with that the wisened little man hobbled out of the bar.

I had a little time to explore Manaus. I'd already been here two days and seen everything there was to see. I'd exhausted my feet looking for anyone who'd heard rumour of the Goddess. Manaus was a rundown little "city" filled with poverty and merchants moving goods up and down the river. Kids played soccer on the roads. The air was alive with sounds of scooters, trucks, cicadas and boisterous people speaking Spanish or Portuguese, I couldn't tell which. There were signs of the Catholic church everywhere but it was night time that this "city" really came alive. People, old and young, loved to dance and sing. Spanish guitar and hand drums were a joy to listen to and all that primal wiggling a joy to behold.

I went to Manaus' old, rundown fort that the Spanish had set up and spent time wondering about the rustic defences of this mighty river. It seemed laughable that old cannons could keep out the mass of life that is the Amazon and Brazil.

"How long will the trip take?" I asked Zarek. He was standing on the peer staring at the sunset, looking out to where the mud met the "clean" water. His boat was tiny. There was enough room for me to lay down at the front, for him to steer at the back and pile some goods in between which he was in the process of doing.

"Your carriage awaits sir," Zarek pointed to the front of the boat. He had thoughtfully provided a blanket for me. It gets cold here at night, "We will be travelling all night,"

"Have you slept?" I was more worried about him falling asleep at the motor as his health.

"Plenty. First $300,"

"Here's $150. The other is for when we meet the Goddess,"

"Ok Mr tough guy. Please take the front,"

I took a seat and pulled the blanket on top of me as much to make me feel brave as to ward off the coming cold. Then Zarek started the motor and steered us into the river.

Sunset is enchanting on the river and the Amazon becomes a symphony of sounds. Animals and birds of every creed wake up to go on the hunt. I saw a king vulture lifting off and a family of sloths slowly moving through the trees.

"Alligators don't bother this boat do they Zarek?" I said trying to sound brave.

"They're called Caimans in the river Marc, they're bigger than alligators and they don't bother us much. But stay out of the water anyway, this is piranha territory," very reassuring.

I watched flights of macaws taking off as well as howler monkeys heading home to sleep. The Amazon is packed with life. As our boat hugged the water I hoped none of it would get too friendly with us, but the sheer beauty of it all!

"Of course, our biggest worry up here is scorpions and millipedes," Zarek informed me, "Some of them get this big," and he held his wide hand apart, "They steal room on the boxes in the boat," I was leaning on a box. Zarek smiled as I tried not to flinch.

The sun set and I tried to sleep but the sounds of the Amazon held me enthralled – or terrified.

Zarek kept talking as I tried to nod off, "You know I take folk like you up the river to meet the Goddess once in a while,"

My blood froze but my voice stayed cool, "You work for her?"

"No, I've never met her, I don't want to. The last man I brought here was a British man 3 months ago. Haven't seen or heard from him since,"

"Then I assume he's Ok," I said in a voice more assured than I felt.

"I assume so ... Sometimes they send a servant to get things from Manaus when they can't make what they need,"

"How many of them are up there?" practicalities to consider.

"I don't know,"

"So no-one has met this Goddess but she's called the Enchanted Woman? Why?"

"Because we see the looks in the eyes of those who come back and never talk," Zarek spelled out, "Try to get some sleep Mr Durwood. You're meeting a Goddess tomorrow," Zarek mocked.

I tried to sleep but every rustle on shore and splash in the water woke me. Eventually, exhausted, I lapsed into a deep sleep.

I dreamt I was ambushed by a golden anaconda. I was squeezed in the coils of the snake but felt no pain. Gold was oozing out from, presumably, my wounds. I looked into the snakes emerald green eyes. I sat up bolt upright in the dark night. Zarek laughed at me. I laid back and watched the canopy of stars overhead, steadied my breath and fell asleep.

Sunrise, another perfect moment on the Amazon where a myriad of bird and animal calls spring to life. I saw golden tamarins and brightly coloured toucans sitting in the trees and Zarek told me that I'd missed some spectacular Caiman and Jaguar action overnight – which made me even more happy.

Zarek took an inlet off the Amazon and suddenly we were floating on clear water.

"Look right Marc. We are now passing the tiny town of Anori. I live there. When you escape, if you escape, if you ever want to, get to the satellite phone and call me. I'll take you back down river," Zarek handed me his number, "Put that number in a very safe place Mr Durwood. I have a feeling you will be needing it,"

We slowly putted past his tiny town and into an even smaller inlet, some miles further up river. The boat came to a stop in some marshy reeds next to a small tin boat.

"Well Mr Durwood this is your last stop. I am a coward and dare go no further. Follow the tiny dirt path South and you can't miss her. Now if you would like to change your mind,"

I smiled, "Thanks Zarek. I guess it's the chosen, brave few from here,"

"Who knows maybe you'll get the gold and the virgins. Maybe,"

I pressed $150 into his hands and got out of his boat. It didn't feel better to be back on dry land. I got my small backpack and looked up that barely trodden path. The only sign that civilised folk had passed this way.

"Good luck Mr Durwood!" Zarek's boat slowly backed away.

"Zarek!"

"Yes?!"

"Could there be bears and cats here?!"

"No bears ... maybe cats and big snakes,"

"Thanks," I waved and watched him pull away.

When he was gone I turned to my only link to civilisation. I got in the tin boat and examined every inch of that motor. I wanted to understand it back to front and with my eyes closed. I started it and the deafening roar made birds flutter and squirrel monkeys scatter in the trees overhead. I turned off the motor and it putted to a stop. I opened my backpack, took out a gun, a Gloc (that I'd only ever practiced about a dozen shots with) and started up that tiny dirt path.

Zarek was right, no bears and thankfully no cats either but long grass and a barely trodden path through it. I thought about anacondas and pumas and how useless my Gloc would be if I was ambushed at this range. I thought about nature in general as it buzzed and hummed and squawked all around me. How unprepared we are for it. How much we think we control it. How much it controls us. How frightening it is when you see it up close. How charming from far away.

The sun had risen now and the heat and sweat was going up and up and up. I took off my jacket and tied it around my waist. I'd travelled about 2 miles (which seems like an age in a jungle when you're scared out of your mind) when I smelt smoke up ahead. My first instinct was civilisation – safety. My next instinct was the Goddess – danger. Perhaps I was going out the frying pan into the proverbial fire but ... I'd come this far.

The jungle began to clear and I was greeted by the sight of rice paddies with long waving stalks. Snakes or cats could easily be in there too. And beyond that a large old brick farmhouse with a few wooden sheds out the back.

I watched parrots take off and saw a poison dart frog on a rice stalk as I tentatively stepped onto those rice paddies. The smoke was coming out of the farmhouse chimney. Clearly the leftovers of last night's fire. I put the Gloc in my backpack and forced myself one foot in front of the other towards the farmhouse.

"What has the outside world brought me?" came the smoothest voice I'd ever heard. I nearly jumped out of my skin. I looked around but saw nothing. "Don't be afraid. Come here boy," I looked in the direction of the voice and that's when I saw one tanned, liquid smooth leg sticking up between the stalks. Then I saw her, about 20 meters away, I could have shot her down right then but that wouldn't have achieved my objective. She was laying on a deck chair sunning herself. She was of average height, about 5ft 8. Her skin was olive to dark and it was hard to tell if she was Brazilian or Indian or both. She was about 30 with wavy black hair just past her shoulders. She wore nothing but a simple yellow shirt which set off her skin and short denim shorts revealing dark and tanned, toned legs. Her skin was smooth and her arms supple and elegant. I stepped over the rice paddies gracelessly. She took her glasses off and I suddenly stopped as I stared into softly burning, emerald eyes. Was this the legendary and dangerous Goddess?

My hand instinctively moved towards my backpack but then her eyes held me. Deep pools of burning and flickering emeralds, a constant stare, half a lifetime of wisdom and experiences burned there. They were captivating.

"Welcome," she smiled through full lips.

I stood there gasping not knowing what to say. Which surprised me a lot.

"Could you take you hand away from your gun please? You're making me nervous,"

"Of course, sorry," her stare was constant and her curious smile held me captive. Her skin could have been the smoothest I'd ever seen. I dropped my hand and then I stepped towards her, "My name is Marc Durwood,"

"Help me up?" she reached one slender hand towards mine. I took her hand and she rose majestically. I kissed her hand! It was wonderful, smooth and warm.

She smiled at my dumbfoundedness, "I see Marc is a civilised gentleman. It's been a while since we've had a new visitor, but I will make you most welcome. Come Marc," she beckoned me with her finger, turned and slowly swayed towards the farmhouse. Her moves were so graceful, the sway of her butt so captivating. How did she do that over the rice fields? My authority was already gone.

"Were you expecting me?"

"We never know when to expect new visitors. The outside world graces us with the presence of men and women from time to time," her gentle coos resonated with my brain and somewhere else as I slowly followed her towards the house, "Your English friend will be pleased to see you,"

"I'm not British,"

"You're American,"

"How can you tell?"

"By your accent and by the fact that you are carrying a gun," her brown legs were long and in perfect shape as she graced over the paddies.

"We don't all carry guns,"

"Just you?"

"It's for the feral animals,"

"You mean native surely. You're the foreign invader here," I felt terrible as we entered the farmhouse.

The small stone room I found myself in was very cosy and homely. Paintings and tapestries from India hung on the wall and a gently crackling fire was dying in the fireplace. Clearly this farmhouse had been made in a different time and had survived long. But what I noticed first were the two, short shorted 20 somethings in the room. One was a short brunette sitting in a comfortable chair by the fireplace. The other was a very tall blonde who was deep in conversation with a squat, balding but robust looking British man.

They stopped talking as we entered.

"Starflower, Amber," the two got up and stood before the Goddess, "This is Marc Durwood he will be staying with us a while. He is armed but doesn't intend to hurt us. Please make him *comfortable* in the spare house," Please say comfortable again Goddess. The Goddess turned to me with those burning eyes, "You will surrender your gun Mr Durwood. We do not allow weapons of any kind here,"

"Of course," I reached into my backpack.

"We'll take care of that in a minute yess," her warm hand on my arm and her yess was a sizzling drill that penetrated and groped for agreement in my brain. I don't think I've ever been more turned on.

"Yes,"

She held out her hand, I took it and kissed it again!

"I'll leave you now in the capable hands of Starflower (a slender arm indicating the blonde) and Amber, "We'll talk more after lunch … Balls," which I thought was a weird thing to say as she stared at me.

"Come with me,"

"Yes my lady," The British man bowed slightly and followed her deeper into the house.

I stared up at Starflower and down at Amber and felt completely humiliated and helpless.

"You won't need a gun here, I assure you," Starflower's eyes were a lovely yellow which gave her the look of a lean lioness.

They both put their hands on my arms and turned me around.

Amber was shapely with short, powerful thighs and lovely brown eyes, "Come," She led the way and I followed them out of the house and the short distance to the roughly built wooden shacks out back.

"This is Mr Balls room," Amber indicated the shack closest to the house, "If you need anything just ask Mr Balls,"

"Balls?" I suppressed a giggle.

"Mr Balls has been a very good guest and a valued friend," piped up Starflower.

"I'm sure he has. But you're not laughing … sorry,"

Amber and Starflower led me to a little, wooden shack round the back and opened the door. "This is your room Mr Durwood," cooed Amber, "Please enter,".

It was a very cosy little room. Rugs on the floors, a wood fire heater, small windows with a lovely view of the fields, a simple but comfortable bed with an Indian patterned bedsheet and no locks on the doors. I thought about commenting on the lock situation, but I had expected this.

"Please make yourself at home," Starflower instructed.

"Lunch will be served at one. We'll leave you to settle in," Amber said. Both of them stared and I was speechless.

Starflower held out her hand, "We'll take your weapon, wallet and mobile phone now. You will have them back when you leave,"

They can have the phone, there's no signal here anyway. I really am on my own now. "Allow me," I said. I took the Gloc from my backpack and removed the clip. I handed both to Starflower along with my wallet and phone. She took the weapon with no fear.

"They'll be kept in the safe in the house. Only the Goddess knows the combination. That way we will all be safe," Starflower said.

"I trust you," I didn't trust them.

"Thank you Mr Durwood," cooed Amber, "There will be a gong to indicate lunch. Until then please settle in,"

"And tour the facilities," Starflower said.

The facilities? She meant this farmhouse and fields?

"We look forward to having you," Starflower smiled along with Amber. I said thanks as they both shut the door behind them. I decided it was time to unpack and have a cigarette.

I don't usually smoke but when in Brazil. I also had this groovy little cigarette lighter I wanted to try out. It was golden and chunky and had cost me a small fortune in Rio. So I puffed on my back porch, which had a hand woven hammock, very civilised, and looked out across the fields. I noticed another little brick building out the back and occasionally a simply dressed Brazilian man would pop in or out. I counted three of them altogether. It was clear that these three worked the house although there really couldn't have been that much to do. One of them hung the laundry and I observed that the Goddess had many ornate dresses (and some risqué underwear). Amber caught me looking at the man hanging laundry and I casually looked away, out over the fields where fruit trees and rice grew. One man was chopping firewood near the Amazon and I thought about how bent his spine must be getting out there on the wet earth.

I finished my cigarette and pocketed my lighter. Starflower did say to tour the facilities. I started with the fields. I said hello to the man chopping firewood with his strong hands who smiled and waved at me but didn't say anything. Clearly the quarters of the servants and Balls were off limits, so I entered the farmhouse. The sun was well up now and with it the humidity. The fire was out in the fireplace so I decided to make myself comfortable in one of the easy chairs. I reflected on how much I'd miss air conditioning. I thought about what must be beyond the hallway leading upstairs. The Goddess' quarters and presumably Amber's and Starflower's. Somewhere up there, presumably, was the safe with my things. I looked around at the tapestries on the wall and listened to the ticking of the clock. Overall it was a very relaxing scene. I got up and entered the simple stone kitchen. Another Brazilian man was in there cooking fresh vegetables and soup. I guess this was lunch. He smiled as I entered.

"Coffee Mr?" he asked. It could have been all the English he knew.

"I'd love one thank you,"

He stopped cutting vegetables to boil the kettle on the wood fired oven. So, this was life off the grid.

"Tea?" he held the tea container up for me which read 'Tea'.

"Actually, tea would be better, thank you,"

I watched the man slowly but calmly preparing lunch and waited for the kettle to boil.

"So how long have you been here?" I asked.

"Sorry, me not speak English,"

"Fair enough,"

He seemed happy enough as he laboured slowly but steadily away. He smiled at me whenever he turned to me.

"Sugar?" he held up the sugar jar reading 'sugar', now he was just showing off.

"No thanks, I'm sweet enough already," and my cheese factor went up another notch.

The metal kettle whistled and the man poured my tea. I thanked him and tasted it. It was amazing! I mean there's tea and teas. I'd had real Chinese tea but this was a step up again! So many subtle fragrances and aromas, I felt like I was walking through a tea plantation. I thanked him again and stepped out the back.

Near the stone building that presumably was the servant's quarters there was a run down little wooden shed. I dared to peek inside.

The door nearly stuck in the mud and I had to work hard to move it at all, but I opened it and inside were farming supplies and everything the house needed to sustain itself tucked away in an orderly manner.

A gong rang somewhere and it was time for lunch. I struggled to close the door. I didn't know where to go so I re-entered the kitchen and offered to help the Brazilian man carry vegetables. He kindly refused, placing his hands together to thank me, but insisted on carrying everything himself. I followed him into the tiny dining room.

"Marc, welcome, you have found us," the Goddess smiled warmly from the head of the simple but well carved wooden table. On either side of her were Amber and Starflower and next to Amber sat Balls.

"Please have a seat," Starflower cooed behind amazing yellow eyes as she got up and offered me the seat beside her.

"Thank you," I smiled as Starflower pushed my seat underneath me. Starflower has lovely, lean and pale legs (I don't know how she avoids a tan down here) and I got to admire them as she slowly slid herself back into place.

The Goddess herself was in a lovely, green Indian dress which really set off her softly burning green eyes, "Amber was afraid you'd lost yourself,"

"Even I would find it hard to lose myself in a place this size," a little insensitive, deliberately, "It is cosy though,"

"It is indeed," smiled Amber with a broad grin. I turned my attention to the man across from me. Squat, round, forbearing and slightly dazed. So this is what 3 months looked like. I stood and offered my hand, "My name's Marc Durwood," he stayed seated but shook my hand firmly, "Glad to know you. My name's Balls, Daniel Balls," so it was catching, "Friends call me Balls or The Balls," he grinned at me broadly. The 3 servants finished bringing in the food and sat next to us. Before us was hearty, chunky soup, fresh bread and vegetables.

"So Balls, how long have you been here?"

"Not quite sure," he laughed, "The days seem to merge together here. Not sure I care,"

"Care to estimate?"

"Balls has been with us for 3 months," I love the way the Goddess says balls. It still resonates with me to this day. Her lovely smile and deep green eyes turned to me and drank me in. I swallowed, "Will you say grace Balls?"

All around the table people linked hands. I took Starflower's smooth, polished perfectly manicured hand on one side and a calloused, dark, middle aged hand on the other. Eyes closed and I followed suit.

"We give thanks to the Goddess of the Earth who provides all our needs and blesses us with each other.

Together through her may we make peace on Earth. Through her will amen,"

"Amen," Starflower squeezed my hand as we woke up.

"Marc you are our most recently arrived guest. Please go first," the Goddess cooed and I almost came.

"Don't mind if I do," I reached into the middle and fished out beans and carrots to grace my soup. I waited until everyone had served themselves and then we ate together. And oh my God the food! The tea had been spectacular and now this! The food was so organic and fresh with subtle flavours and spices! I'd had nothing like it. Typically, I had dinners for one from a supermarket packet.

"This is extraordinary!" I commented. The Goddess' eyes rolled to me with a smile that ate me up. I felt daft that I had broken the silence.

"Mmmm, there is nothing but fresh vegetables here," Amber said smoothly, "The toxins of the world's foods will soon be washed away from you," Amber's liquid brown eyes held mine, but I couldn't take my eyes off the Goddess who was still staring at me.

"We believe in a clean and natural diet," Starflower's voice throbbed as she explained. Her hand delicately touched my leg below my shorts, "No outside additives, preservatives or colours are allowed to touch our food,"

"You see Marc there is nothing artificial here," the Goddess sighed, "Nature has given us everything we need. Nature did not give us mobile phones or models on billboards or guns because we never needed them,"

"I agree she has," I commented as the presence of Starflower's hand made me bar up below, "This is all-natural food?"

"Nothing but the goodness of the garden," Amber smiled.

"Spices you've never tasted, all the way down," Starflower rested her hand on my knee and her yellow eyes bored down into mine. I swallowed.

"It is extraordinary," I commented. They all smiled, except the servants who couldn't understand what I was saying.

"Eat as much as you like Marc," the Goddess cooed and I wanted to eat it all, "It's all healthy," This wasn't going well, they were getting to me. I was aware of incense burning nearby but couldn't see the source. The aroma was quite relaxing.

After lunch the servants got up first, bowed and cleared away the dishes.

"I've never eaten like that and I've eaten in Paris," I smiled at my hostesses.

"And you'll find Marc that as the toxins of the world leave you, you'll become more and more clearheaded," the Goddess' eyes bored into me and I wasn't sure whether to believe her.

"We were all born to be free of the toxins of the world," Starflower assured me, "Including the toxins of news, TV and entertainment,"

"I agree," Kammil would have approved, "Some TV is good,"

"Some," The Goddess rose which was a sight to behold by itself. It was majestic, like she was getting up from a body of water, "Marc, will you take a walk with me in the gardens?"

"Of course Goddess," and I got up quickly. Balls waved at me as I followed the Goddess.

I exited behind the Goddess through the door and into the gardens. I thought she was being glib about the gardens but indeed there were some. A vegetable garden stretching far into the fields that I had missed on my "tour" around the house. But could they really sustain themselves just through this?

"Does this really supply all you need? I mean I'm impressed. You seem very self-sufficient here,"

"No one is self-sufficient Marc, we are all interconnected, even here," she smiled up at me.

"Then how do you get what you need from the outside world?"

"Whenever we have need of the outside world I send Aba to the nearby village or sometimes he goes all the way to Manaus," she stretched her majestic arm out, "Then we have visitors like yourself who connect us to the outside world,"

"You never leave this place Goddess?"

"Why would I Marc? I have everything I need. Young virile men around me to do the work. I couple of apprentices to keep me company and the freshest food in the most peaceful location in the world,"

"You never get bored?" I smiled.

She smiled warmly back, "Why would I Marc? I have you all to keep me entertained," and she winked, I swallowed again.

I followed her through the garden into the rice fields. Her green dress was short which gave way to her tanned, sturdy and well-defined legs. It was amazing that she could float across the mud so gracefully as I squelched behind her.

"Walk next to me Marc. I don't want you walking behind me,"

"Sorry my Goddess," and I moved beside her, "Is it because of the gun?"

"Yes,"

"I'm sorry about that. It was for the animals,"

"You Americans find security in guns?"

"The whole world does. It's not just us. I don't often trudge through the Amazon alone,"

"Your gun would not stop nature for long Marc," she stared at me.

"A decent enough bang would scare away most animals. Your own little enclave seems to be doing well enough at keeping nature away,"

"We live in harmony with nature. We do not fight against it," it was joy watching her wavy black hair bob along and the sturdy grace of her legs. Not to mention her softly, burning eyes. There was no fighting nature here.

"No, I can see that,"

"And you will find Marc that despite your fears nature is, in the end, the only way to be,"

"Now I believe that," she knew about my fears?

"But not the rest of what I say?"

"You seem like a woman of great wisdom,"

We walked in silence for a way.

I took out a cigarette and the lighter and started to puff.

"You must be kidding Marc. No toxins next to my body,"

"No of course. I'm sorry," and I stubbed the cigarette out.

"Frankly I'm surprised you smoke," the Goddess began, "You seem a most healthy man."

"Old habits die hard …"

"You certainly will. You would do well to give it up while you're here,"

"I'll work on it,"

"Do that. No smoking in the house and only next to your lodgings, not inside them,"

"Naturally Goddess,"

"Naturally, I like that. Did you always carry a gun Marc?"

"No, only since being led off the beaten track. I had a very normal life once,"

"Did you enjoy this *normal life*?"

"I liked it yes,"

"I didn't ask if you liked it Marc. I asked if you *enjoyed* it,"

"Well no,"

"Something was missing?" her luminous eyes searched me.

"A certain … satisfaction,"

"You lived apart from nature Marc. How else could you expect to feel? And you're not just talking about sex Marc. The whole *process* just felt wrong,"

"I'm … starting to see why the world is so off colour,"

"Starting to," the Goddess smiled, "You are not a violent man, I can see that. Balls on the other hand must unlearn bad habits of the world,"

"He's a violent man?"

"A lovely man who used to serve in the army," her eyes held mine and I swallowed.

"Look I'm sorry about the gun. I didn't mean to scare anybody,"

"You didn't scare anybody and it is forgivable. It is just your *tension* Marc," I loved the way she said tension, it rippled through me, "It is clear you do not trust easily,"

"Isn't that a good thing?"

"An understandable habit from a mixed-up world. You will come to trust all of us implicitly," I wondered if she was right.

"Forgive me Goddess, we have just met,"

"Why did you come here Marc?" her eyes were like a warm fire searching me.

"I … met a few of your … disciples. They opened my eyes to many things,"

"That's not why you're here,"

"… No,"

"Tell me Marc," her eyes implored.

"I want my freedom,"

"You're in the right place Marc," the Goddess smiled warmly, "You want freedom from the world or freedom to the world?" That confused me, "Either way the answer is the same. You're free now Marc,"

"Yes,"

"And yet you came here anyway seeking something else,"

"Yes … no … I … it's complicated,"

"No Marc, like most things it's very simple,"

"I admit when I heard you were down here I was a bit curious,"

"A bit?" the Goddess smiled and I thought I'd dive into those eyes right there, "Ok Marc it's clear that we can help each other, to grow," she put her hand gently on my arm. Oh ask me to grow again Goddess! "Rest now, you are among friends yess?"

"Yes," I said and she waited for me to say, "friends,"

"Take a rest, dinner is served at 6," she smiled and walked away from me. I watched her sway, her hair bob and her legs carry her gracefully towards the house. I didn't know what else to do, so I obeyed. I went back to my room, breathed calm into my libido and took a rest on the comfortable bed. Tension suddenly evaporated I soon fell into a very comfortable sleep.

After dinner it was getting dark, so I went onto the back porch and smoked another cigarette. I felt so invigorated. I wondered about how much the smoke was damaging me but so be it. At least it was a habit to keep me anchored to the real world. Wherever that was. Balls was lazing in his woven hammock watching the sunset which I had to admit was sensational. Amber was there talking to him. He waved at me, but they kept to themselves. There was a light wind that rustled the rice stalks in the fields and my hair. The whole scene was so natural and I wondered about what the Goddess had said about nature. My own apartment in the city was surrounded by other apartments and noisy traffic. I had a pot plant but it was the furthest thing away from places like this. I had a lot to thank the Sisterhood for. I went to sleep that night and dreamed comfortable dreams.

I dreamt of Amanda and Iris and Rachelle. I was in a pinball machine and I was the pinball. Amanda, Rachelle and Iris were naked giants whacking me around the table and I was bouncing off the obstacles. I loved it. They were laughing, I was laughing. I felt wild and free. Other Sisterhood members represented obstacles and I bounced happily off Silvia and Marie, Cassandra and Gina, Adelene and Cecile and Karla. Suddenly Amanda missed and I fell towards the gaping hole at the bottom and I just knew I was falling towards the Goddess, "Welcome," she said and all went black. I wanted to wake up but couldn't. I stayed in the black as I became aware of pleasure gradually building in my member. I groaned.

Someone was sucking me with power and subtlety. "Go with it," said a voice into my ear and I smiled with joy.

Slowly I was waking up. Curiously the sensation down below was actually increasing.

I became aware of the ceiling above me, the blanket covering me and the smooth and intense joy happening below me. I raised my head and looked down and there she was. Starflower had my legs firmly in place with her wide mouth encompassing me in a joyful embrace. Her tongue rippled on me and she rose up and down on me in smooth and warm motions. She sat up and smiled at me with clear blue eyes which was a bit of a shock (she must have worn yellow contacts yesterday), "Good morning Marc. It is another beautiful day, yes a beautiful day," she bent down and her smooth mouth encompassed me. I sighed and my head went back. Her tongue worked up and down on me in slow, deliberate circles. She drew off me, she was better than anyone I'd ever had.

"Do we wake up like this every morning?" I asked from a place of bliss.

"No, only when we have special guests,"

"I'm not that special," I said as special lips lowered delicately on again.

She slid herself off and smiled down at my member, "I disagree,".

Another wonderful day in the Sisterhood had begun.

We all ate together at the table for breakfast. It was 3 square meals a day with our set positions. Except this morning, "Marc sit next to me," the Goddess pointed one braceleted hand at the seat Starflower usually adopted. I sat next to the Goddess and Starflower slid in next to me. Starflower placed a hand on my leg and kept it there. Balls smiled at me knowingly and Amber smiled warmly.

"Did you sleep well Marc?" asked the Goddess coolly.

"Like a baby and boy did I rise up this morning,"

Balls almost lost his food.

"Good Marc. As in nature we all need a good night sleep and the prospect of joy," the Goddess' voice throbbed and resonated deep inside of me. I silently agreed.

"So, what's on the cards today?" I said.

"After breakfast you will come with me," the Goddess smiled. I silently looked forward to it.

"Did you sleep well Balls?" I asked. I became further aware of Starflower's hand on my leg, gently squeezing me.

"Always," he replied and smiled at me. The three servants ate silently at the end of the table.

"Balls rested next to me last night," Amber cooed, "He slept like a baby," and she brushed the back of his neck.

"Like a baby," Balls repeated from bliss. I trembled.

"Did you have pleasant dreams Marc?" the Goddess' eyes bored into me.

It was at that moment I felt Amber's (I assume it was Amber's) foot make contact with my naked leg.

"The dreams were wonderful. And waking up even better," I made eye contact with Amber.

"What did you dream?" the Goddess asked.

Amber's foot slowly rose on my leg and then settled deep into the core of me. Her foot rose and fell majestically, stroking deep love into me.

"I … don't remember," I lied. I wasn't going to give them my dreams, "I do remember waking up though," I smiled up at Starflower who smiled back.

"A dream *come* true you could say?" could the Goddess say come again please?

"Yes you could say that,"

We ate fresh fruit and oats in silence. I was told that toxins were leaving my body and I believed it. Balls was in bliss on his neck and I was in increasing bliss down below. Starflower ran her hand down my leg, electrifying me. Starflower stood up, "I have chores to attend to my Goddess,"

"Very good dear," Starflower left, "Marc, when you are ready please come upstairs. Amber will show you the way. I have something to show you,"

"Yes my Goddess," the Goddess rose and I admired her form under her simple black dress. She left me with Amber gracing me slowly down below, and the servants gradually clearing things away.

"So ..." I started. Amber regarded me coolly, "how long have you been here Amber?"

"I'm not entirely sure Marc," such penetrating brown eyes, such a firm and subtle foot, "Time is fluid here,"

"I'm sure it's not the only thing that's fluid,"

"That's true. Does it matter?" her foot was convincing me it didn't.

"Where are you from Amber?"

"Now, now, it's not polite to ask a woman's location," and her toes squeezed me subtly below. From her accent I guessed US west coast.

"It's not like I asked your age," it was hard to talk as Amber suddenly worked me harder under the table. She has a talented big toe and she rolled it up and down, up and down.

"I do know I've been here a *long* time," she smiled at me as her foot stroked me to heaven. My heart rate went up. Did they know? Then her foot relaxed me.

I finished my breakfast which like everything else here was organic and gorgeous. I reflected that I was nervous as to what was waiting for me upstairs but also that I wanted to go. "Shall we go," I said, "Don't want to keep the Goddess waiting long," her foot ran down me one last time and withdrew. I shiver went up my spine, "Indeed we don't," she agreed.

I followed Amber into a tiny corridor and then onto a narrow but carpeted set of stairs. As we climbed I couldn't help but admire Amber's short but sturdy and toned brown thighs working away under her firm butt. She wore a short black skirt and light brown top that really set off her eyes. It wasn't her eyes I was looking at now though as we ascended the stairs and I watched her calves work away at them one after the other. Reaching the top Amber bade me go through to the room beyond and bowed low, "This way sir," she said with dramatic effect.

I entered into a cosy space with a slanted roof, a simple desk and the Goddess in her ornate green dress staring at two paintings on the wall. She ignored me as I entered. Eventually I cleared my throat.

"Marc come over here," the Goddess waved me over, "Tell me what you think of this?"

I was looking at an extremely well-drawn painting but what really caught me was the subject. I was looking at a fiery apocalyptic landscape and on that was a pyramid. No ordinary pyramid – one made out of people. At the bottom hundreds and hundreds of what looked like slaves in their tattered clothes bent their backs and seemed to be struggling to hold up the pyramid and propel the whole thing forward. On the next level sat men in suits slaving on computers and tired and weary, shouting priests who held up the next level which was made up of men in immaculate suits eating a fine lunch which held up the fourth and final level: One man with a hooked nose sat at the top with a black suit and crooked hat. He had a steering wheel, a whistle tube to shout at the people and an accelerator which ended in an electric prod for the people below.

There were other pyramids all scooting around the landscape. Some collided like dodgem cars sending sprays of slaves into the air. The people at the top seemed to be having a hilarious time. Some people at the bottom had fallen over exhausted and were ground under hundreds of feet as pyramids ran over them.

"These were a gift from an apprentice of mine who showed great promise," the Goddess cooed.

"She painted them herself?"

"She did," a quick look at the signature read Karla Hardings, "Come and look at this one," the Goddess beckoned me with her finger and I followed her to the next painting.

Same pyramids except this time they were lined up in a row. Three of them each charging in the same direction - towards a cliff. The first one was running as normal with the man at top and slaves running the pyramid as fast as they brokenly could at the bottom. The second pyramid was closer to the abyss and the man at the top was strapping on what appeared to a jet pack. Below him were what I assumed were politicians putting on gold coloured parachutes. The rest just didn't notice the cliff they were running towards. One slave did and was trying to warn the others. No-one could hear him and he looked like he was going to get crushed. The third pyramid was off the edge of the cliff. Hundreds of slaves were falling into the abyss. A man at his computer typed unaware that he was falling. A priest yelled and faced the heavens. The politicians opened their golden parachutes and sank slowly into the abyss as the leader of the pyramid got away on his smoke belching jet pack.

"What do you think?" the Goddess asked me.

"Very poignant,"

"But do you appreciate what it means?" she cooed.

"I think the symbolism is hard to miss,"

"But how did he do it?"

"Eh?"

"How did one man convince 99 men to commit suicide,"

"They didn't know they were running towards a cliff,"

"The information was staring them in the face,"

"... Please tell me how he did it,"

"You just don't want to say, do you Marc?"

"Hypnosis,"

"Conditioning. Sociological conditioning from a very early age,"

"Corporations?" I ventured.

"No ... the world. Look again Marc and tell me is this not the world you've always known," I looked again and I had to agree it seemed a fairly accurate picture of the world.

"This world has always existed," the Goddess assured me, "At least the first painting," she guided me back to pyramids playing dodgem cars, "One, usually a man, at the top steering millions into each other or starvation or both," she guided me back to the second painting, "This one was sent to me years after she left. It seems she'd updated her ideas to encompass what she feels is the end of the world,"

"She has a case," I conceded, "There's a number of ways the world could end now. We survived nuclear war ...""

"If we survive nuclear war," the Goddess corrected, "the threat is now *larger* than ever,"

"If we survive nuclear war," I repeated, "then there's environmental collapse. If we survive that then there's the advent of general AI,"

"And if we survive that," the Goddess said, "there is the rise of oligarchy around the world,"

"They've always been there," I stared at the man powering away on his jetpack, the commander of the butchering of millions.

"It is the world we've left behind," she waved her hand dismissively at the paintings.

"I must admit I've thought about leaving the world a few times myself,"

"Marc Durwood the hermit," the Goddess laughed, "I don't think so,"

"Why not? You've done it,"

"You care too much. And I am not a hermit thank you very much. I have a whole community here,"

"A pretty small one,"

"It's getting *larger*," the Goddess' green eyes enveloped me and indeed it was getting larger, "I have quite the following around the world. I'm sure you're aware of that,"

"But you're scarcely a part of it. Why did you withdraw from the community?"

"Not I, my mother withdrew from the community more than 30 years ago. She withdrew to get away from that," she pointed to the paintings, "She could see which way the world was heading and decided to create an organic community with those who wanted to live organically," those eyes, so inviting.

"I didn't want to. Your people just pulled me into this,"

"Do you regret it? Having your eyes opened,"

"No, I've seen a lot of what is horrible and beautiful in the world. I wouldn't trade it for anything,"

"Then why are you really here Marc?"

I stumbled on my words. I couldn't tell her I wanted to leave. Especially looking at those paintings. To go back to that! The Goddess smiled at me warmly and put her hand on my hand, so warm!

"Let me show you why you came," I looked into her eyes and saw the whole world in there. I thought I'd died and gone to heaven. I thought I could stay in there forever. Perhaps I could.

The Goddess slowly walked away and I watched her sway as she smiled back at me. I went to follow but a hand on my shoulder stopped me, "Wait here please," I had forgotten Amber completely! "The Goddess needs time to prepare," the Goddess disappeared behind a curtain of beads, "You'll be in there soon enough," I looked with nervous excitement and wanted to dive in there right now! "Let's spend a bit of time together while you wait," Amber giggled whilst holding my hand. I stared down into Amber's brown eyes and wanted to dive straight into a second-rate Goddess (no insult intended). I took a deep breath to calm down. I should have expected this and needed to control myself.

Amber led me across the room and I shook myself awake slightly thinking that perhaps my gun was hidden around here. "Have a seat," Amber instructed and I sat on a low and very comfortable couch. Amber moved slowly around the space. I could hear what seemed to be Indian chants along with African drums coming from the inner sanctum that I was destined to enter. I looked at Amber's powerful little legs as she retrieved some incense and lit it by the windowsill. Now I was watching Amber's legs and large breasts, bobbing shoulder length hair and breathing in musty perfumed air whilst listening to calm Indian music.

"Are you trying to relax me or put me to sleep Amber?"

"Which would you like?" Amber smiled knowingly as she prepared two hot drinks. She walked over to me making that klick clacking sound I loved now on the wooden floor. I looked up at her towering over me. The top of two brown breasts rolled into view. "Drink this," she offered me an ornate cup filled with brown liquid. "What is it?" I asked.

"It's tea. It will help you relax,"

"Do I need to be more relaxed?" I took the cup from her. Amber sat on a bean bag across from me. She crossed her exceptional legs. "I don't know Marc you've seemed a little *tense* since you got here,"

"You've got to admit that this is not your average home," I took a sip and enjoyed the steam on my face. Very soothing.

"No ... but it could be," she was serious. I looked to the beads wondering with excitement and some trepidation what was waiting beyond for me, "You're in safe hands Marc. Relax,"

"I believe that," and I pretty much did.

Amber slowly ran a hand down her calf and a shiver went up my spine. Not a scared shiver but a joyful, sexy shiver. I took another sip of the exquisite tea. I really should let myself go with this.

"Believe it," Amber instructed and I stared into her powerful brown eyes. This was joy beyond joy.

"Like everything else here, this is extraordinary," I sighed and sank a little deeper in the couch, "What type of tea is it?"

"Lijiang high mountain tea," Amber's voice throbbed which seemed to boom comfortably in my ear, "Picked at the dawn of Spring in the coldest weather at the top of a very high mountain. Virgin leaves make the perfect drink,"

So there were virgins, "Perfect yes?" I asked.

"Perfect," Amber's voice purred in my ear and I sank a little lower. Her hand tapped her knee and my eyes were drawn there. She really is in exquisite shape.

I took another sip of the rain water and tea and saw Amber make slow circles on her knee through the smoke. The gentle hum of Indian chants, African drums and slow gongs was relaxing my mind and I thought why not look.

"You're in extraordinary shape Amber," wait did I mean to say that? Who cares?

"Thank you Marc. I've got to admit you're quite the man yourself,"

"Thank you," her hand became a slow constant rub up and down her exquisite calf and thigh. She massaged deep into the muscles of her calf and my eyes were comfortably fixed.

"And there's no reason you shouldn't enjoy yourself Marc," Amber's voice resonated in my brain, "People deserve joy,"

"The world needs more of it,"

"Indeed," I was barely aware of the tea I was drinking anymore. Just fingers on polished calf and that skin and that voice!

"Just let yourself *sink* in Marc," I breathed out and did, "Let the natural rhythm take you," I watched her hands on her thigh as she squeezed tension out of her muscles and out of me with her voice. I listened to that incredible relaxing drum music which seemed so close now, "Relax Marc," she breathed and I did. I could have fallen asleep right there with the biggest hard on I'd had in quite a while.

"Marc," Amber got up, came over and sank into the seat beside me. She put a hand on my face and turned me to face her lovely eyes, 'Marc, you're a leg man aren't you?"

"Seem to be,"

"Put your hands on my thighs," I did, "Rub," I rubbed and breathed in deep relaxation. So polished, so exquisite, so fitting with this music and perfumed air. "Marc," her hand moved to my crotch, "Would you like a blow job while you wait?"

Would I! But what I said was "Aghhhh," Amber's hand gently grasped and stroked up the length of me and then she was fishing inside my jeans. Somewhere from a place of bliss my jeans had come undone and she held me firmly, stroking ever upwards with her hands while her eyes held me and she licked her lips.

I watched Amber slowly lower herself down as she said, "Hmmmmm," at the heart of me, setting off a huge squirt of dopamine in my brain and reverberated through my bursting member.

Then with that Indian chanting playing and tea on my breath, she slowly lowered herself on. It was an extraordinary feeling. Her tongue was short but extremely passionate as she licked all over me. She slowly slid her mouth up and down, up and down and then sucked and swallowed. I thought I'd come right there and thought about the Goddess waiting for me. Then the sucking became too powerful. My head went back and I'm sure I spilled my tea. I remember thinking I was grateful the cup didn't break. Amber's mouth was so powerful! Her thighs were so powerful! Everything here was so powerful!

Slowly Amber removed herself and stood above me. "Marc," Amber caressed my face as I stared at those all-powerful eyes, "The Goddess will see you now," Amber helped me stand. I don't remember doing up my trousers but they were. I stumbled in the direction of the music, the beads and the Goddess beyond.

I parted the beads and stepped into a small but intimate space. Tapestries lined the walls. The gentle rhythmic drums reverberated softly around my head. The smell of the air was gorgeous, sweet and musky as the incense burned. And there, sitting on a collection of brightly coloured cushions was the Goddess. She had changed. She wore exquisite Indian jewels, a few bits of elegant cloth and little else. Tassels covered her most intimate parts but that was all. She had what appeared to be a sapphire in the middle of her forehead and an Indian crown that sparkled on her head. I approached this vision slowly. Her movements were slow, relaxed and so fluid with her eyes constantly fixed on me.

"Come and sit Marc," she stroked the cushion next to herself.

"Is it ok?" I stood before this powerful, mostly naked and firm vision.

"Why wouldn't it be Marc?" the Goddess breathed, "Sit," I slowly lowered myself next to this Goddess. I was a little below her and she smiled down on me with cool, softly burning green eyes. My hands were level with her delicately folded, tanned and toned thighs.

"Marc you did come here to find freedom but you'll find that freedom has a different meaning to what you previously believed," Her hand held my chin and I was gazing up into burning eyes, "Are you ready to experience the freedom that you sought?" the Goddess cooed.

"Do I have a choice?" I said from somewhere.

"Yes you do. We could sit here for an hour or two and have a nice conversation or you can discover what you really came here for,"

"Take me there," I said on autopilot.

"Good choice," the Goddess eyes penetrated me as she stroked my face.

"What do you think of the aromas Marc?" I breathed in deeply and enjoyed the musk, "It's heavy,"

"Heavy, I like that,"

"I feel like the air is viscous and pushing against me," the Goddess' hands began running over my chest and back. She undid my buttons expertly, all the whilst her softy burning eyes on me. She peeled the shirt from my back, "And the music?" she asked. The drums and chants reverberated around my soul. "Primal," I breathed out. "Primal, yesss," her hand went up and brushed over my head, "Breath in the heavy aromas Marc," I did and it was satisfying. Was her forehead ruby starting to glow? Her arms came around me and supported my lungs. "Deep breath in," I obeyed, "And out. In and out," Her firm hands held the bottom of my ribs and the heady atmosphere felt good. I felt so supported looking into those deep green eyes. The drumming entered my soul, "Deep breath in … and out," I relaxed further. Her hands were so warm and the drumming so peaceful and yet powerful, awaking something in my soul, something primal.

"Marc, you're a good boy," the Goddess stroked my face as I looked up into those deep green eyes, "Marc stand," I did. The Goddess sat up and one firm hand wrapped around my butt as the other worked the buttons on my pants. Her feet wrapped around my legs and held me in place as she gently pulled my trousers down around my ankles, "Sit," I sat with the Goddess' legs wrapping me as she pulled my trousers from myself and tossed them in the corner. Now I was sitting before this Goddess in only Y fronts. Her hands brushed over the muscles of my chest and arms. "Marc place your hands on me," "Where?" I can't believe I was waiting for instructions. "Why don't you start with my torso?". Like in a dream I reached forward and touched this Goddess on her exposed abdomen, "Good Marc," I rubbed slowly and gently, she was smooth and firm. My hands brushed her sides and back. The Goddess took my hands and moved them up to her breasts. I gently squeezed the rounded joys through those tiny bits of cloth. Firm but yielding, I was in heaven. Her thigh came over my shoulder and suddenly I was held firmly in place. I started shifting, "No don't panic," the Goddesses eyes held me, "Just relax,"

"What was in that tea you gave me?" I asked from a far away place.

"Just something to help you relax and to open your mind," did the ruby on her forehead start to sparkle more brightly? "Just breath in Marc and listen to my voice,"

"As if I could do anything else,"

She smiled down on me with a warm smile and her other leg came around my shoulder holding me firmly in place. She gently squeezed the sides of my neck. My hands instinctively moved to her legs to stop her. So smooth!

"Cheeky boy," the Goddess admonished, "Well now that I have your hands on my legs I might as well use them. Rub me," I loved the way she said rub me, a command that could make me come. I moved my hands slowly up and down her polished legs. Polished marble entered my fingertips which melded with the smoke and deep melodic sounds.

"So you're a Goddess huh?"

"That's right,"

"Can you prove it?"

"All in good time dear boy," the Goddess stroked my face and forced me to look up at her. I already believed her, I just wanted her to prove it. She reached up and delicately removed the cloth over her chest. Sumptuous breasts rolled into view. I lunged gently at them but couldn't move from the legs squeezing my neck. The Goddess's head went back as she squeezed her own breasts. This teasing was more than I could bare. The primal music was getting to me and I clawed at the thighs wrapping my head. The Goddess laughed, "Wait dear boy," She rubbed a fingertip around her nipple and then she delicately pushed the polished fingertip onto my lip. She moved my lips aside and pushed her fingertip deep inside my mouth. I sucked and sucked and gently bit on it instinctively. She withdrew her finger, rubbed the next one on her nipple and inserted that in my mouth. I'm sure her forehead sapphire was glowing by now. And did I feel something else? A third and fourth hand close around me. I couldn't look down but I felt like I was being massaged by eight arms, all hers as they gently massaged my sides. She slid her finger from my mouth. Her legs released me and I looked down. There were the eight Goddess arms stroking me.

I gazed up at her trying to figure it all out.

"Just relax Marc. It will make sense with time,"

Fuck that! I was being held by a ten-armed Goddess! "Don't ever let me go," I said. "I won't," the Goddess reassured me and her arms stroked love into my torso. She spread her many arms and suddenly my arms and legs became enveloped in her loving embrace. She rubbed deep calm into all of me. Her ruby glowed as I gazed into her amazing eyes.

"You really are a Goddess,"

"I am," her strokes massaged deep love into my head, arms, shoulders, chest and legs, "Kiss me," I did as instructed and found soft lips parting their ways to heavens that I had only dreamt about. Her lips were soft and her tongue penetrating my mouth and brain to higher pleasures no mortal had ever experienced before. I freed an arm and stroked her face, "I always knew you were real," I said.

"How did you know?"

"I just knew,"

"I am," she smiled down on me. One of her arms found my penis and wrapped around. She pulled up and down, up and down. My eyes rolled back into heaven, "Long," she began, and my head reeled, "Such a long boy and so much longing for this," her fingers teased me and I thought I'd come right there. Her fingers pinched the end of my dick and I throbbed back come, "Wait for me boy," she instructed brushing my face.

"Yes Goddess," and I subsided, "How are you doing this?" I asked from somewhere blissful and her arms gently stroked me off to heaven. Two of her arms took my arms and moved them to circle her waist. I rubbed up her smooth back. "Undo my cloth," she instructed.

"I'm not sure I can," I giggled my fingers were tingling and the Goddess undid the scarf wrapped around her waist. She pushed my head forward with two of her hands encompassed my face and pulled me down into those mountains. They firmly but softly yielded to my face. I sucked slowly and hard on the long nipples.

"Longing," began the Goddess as she stroked slow love into my dick, "Such a longing for this," I sucked softly on heavenly nipples, "How long have you waited to live," she breathed into my ear. I kissed down her torso, heading for her inner core. I peeled away the bottom sash slowly with my teeth and tossed it aside.

"Not yet boy," I waited. Two hands wrapped into my Y fronts and I helped step out of them until I was naked before her as she was before me.

"Marc Durwood, now are you ready for your freedom and enter heaven?"

"YES!!"

"Then part my lips and blow," she pushed me down on her with four strong arms. She rubbed over my shaft and the rest of me as my tongue slid out and into the Goddess. Her head fell back as her arms massaged me and I massaged and served my Goddess. My tongue slid inside her and I felt the juiciest heaven. I wanted to serve her forever. Two of her arms held my head but I wanted to stay inside her forever. I'm not sure how much time passed as we lounged like this on the cushions, but this indeed was freedom. Eventually, "Man come up," and her hands gently pulled me up to gaze into those deep green eyes. Her 10 arms drew circles over my flesh and neck, "Are you free?"

"Yes, yes I am," I sighed. The Goddess licked her lips and slowly kissed down my torso. All ten arms circled my waist and legs.

Her heavenly mouth was in front of my member as she held me. "Marc, you are about to enter a covenant with me. You serve me any time I want and in return I take you closer and closer," she breathed on my twitching cock, "to enlightenment. Do you agree?"

I thought about it for a second that seemed like years as she blew warm air on my cock, "I agree,"

And then heaven really started. Her lips touched me and slowly I disappeared deep inside her. Joy pulsated up my throbbing cock, her mouth slowly pulsed and licked. The drums and incense entered my mind and I felt her tongue enter my brain. Like a lick of fire from my cock to my brain she seemed to be sucking life into me. For an insanely long time it seemed we lay like this. Me watching patterns swirl on the ceiling and in the smoke as my cock, body and mind entered higher and higher enlightenment. Then she finally drew slowly off and I wanted to beg her to jump back on. She was kissing up my torso again. Her arms working up me as she went. She came up to my head and I kissed her now brightly glowing ruby.

"Deep inside me boy now," she whispered in my ear as she slowly climbed over me. My member felt her parting lips and then she slowly lowered herself onto me. My cock entered 12th heaven. 10 arms held her above me as she worked me slowly but evenly up and down, up and down. All parts of her brushing against me and held me tantalisingly close to coming. She seemed to know exactly when I was going to come and would stop. I'd be in agony and she stroked love and cooled me back with her gentle words in my ear. I gazed into those softly burning pools as she rode me gently. I'm not sure how long I'd been inside her when she finally released me and let me come. Her smiling face encompassed me as I reached out for heaven. I came closer to enlightenment.

Later we just held each other and her ten arms gradually faded away into two. We rubbed each other's polished skin and I kissed the Goddess' neck.

"Have you found what you were looking for?" the Goddess' eyes held me.

"Yes. This is freedom," she stroked my face.

"Enlightenment," she smiled.

Later I laid on my bed thinking over what had happened. Clearly I had had a profound spiritual experience brought on by drugs but what an experience! And how did she know my trigger word 'long,'? Clearly, I would need to rethink my position here. Maybe she really was a Goddess. I even forgot to have a smoke that night, I was so wrapped in this amazing, extra-sensory woman. Was she the real thing?

From there days turned into weeks and weeks probably turned into months. I say probably because time seems to move fluidly here. Sometimes faster, sometimes slower. The watch I'd brought with me was in the valuables safe with all my personal effects. As if you couldn't trust the people here, of course you could. The Goddess kept everyone on a very comfortable leash.

So, every now and again I'd wake up like this – Starflower or Amber or once even the Goddess herself would tap into my dreams with the greatest blow jobs known to man. I'd wake up moaning in the raptures of heaven, eager for another day in the Sisterhood. The Goddess made the rounds. She'd see Balls and myself perhaps a couple of times a week (it's hard to tell really) and lift us to astrosex heaven. Each session seemed stronger than the last and I really felt I was approaching greater knowledge each time. I had let go of a lot of bad ideas. The bad idea of artificial time was gone. I was now free to live naturally by the rise and fall of the sun. It felt much better and relaxed than constantly looking at a watch. I was grateful that they had taken it away. The bad idea of processed food was gone. I enjoyed the taste of everything grown in nature. Our staple was rice and occasionally bread. And if you don't believe me when I say organic food is much better than the slop we get out of the supermarket I say this. Buy some processed orange juice, drink it wait some time then squeeze a *real* orange into a glass and drink *that* – you'll get the idea, only much better. I felt healthier, younger, less stressed and my palette was full of subtle aromas and tastes with every meal. I felt much fitter than I'd felt in years. And that's because both Balls and myself were helping out. We did some chores around the house along with the three locals Aba, Gambino and Ualtar who were most charming men you could ever meet. Balls wasn't bad either. The three servants weren't left out either. Once a week the Goddess would take each of them upstairs and "lift their consciousness and spirits,". Everyone was happy. Amber and Starflower were gradually increasing in power which was a joy to behold and Balls and myself would tend the fields, cut the firewood and mend the house. I couldn't remember the last time I'd done manual work and the joy which came from being outside in genuine fresh air surrounded by a jungle full of the symphony of animal and bird sounds. We'd play games and have discussions to pass the time in the evenings. This was community, this was joy, this is what life could be, this is what life should be. No phones, no billboards, no keeping up with the Jones. This was the wisdom of the elders, the natives who lived this way for so many years before we came along and ruined it all.

The greatest toxin I let go of was the idea of the 40 hour week. That prison where the drones showed up for work, whined, bitched and moaned for an unnatural 40 hours. Nothing got done but grown stress cancers and return home to collapse when they should have been living life. I lived the life of a free man, not a working camel, or a simple slave tied to an uncaring machine. These people did care, I was getting closer to nature every day and nature's burden was light and there was real and plentiful *reward.*

Still a couple of things bothered me or at least confused me. The Goddess was a woman, right? Just a woman. She wasn't really be a Goddess. Then how did she know my trigger word and how did she say it with such sexiness? The drug in the tea I took gladly, it enriched the experience but that didn't explain how constantly her eight other arms emerged and the sapphire in her forehead glowed. Once I even hallucinated that the sapphire opened and a beautiful and infinitely peaceful and knowing third eye stared down at me. How did she do that? Asking her didn't get anywhere. She just informed me that I was becoming more enlightened and this was how human beings naturally were. Maybe she really was a Goddess. Either way I was closer to nature and the heavens than I'd ever hoped to be. This was real life.

And I still had the occasional cigarette despite the Goddess' suggestions to give them up. These cigarettes were now the only link to my old life. I thought about giving them up too but I always found a reason to keep putting it off. I guess a part of me still wanted that commercially crass world out there.

It was a day like any other except I woke up with Starflower's tongue wrapped around my member and her pussy in my face. What a way to wake up with a nubile demi-goddess straddling me, pinning me down with her thighs on either side of my head, her pussy in my face and my member so *deep* inside her. My tongue emerged straight away and I heard her moan on top of me. I forced my hands out of the bed and grabbed the firm tissues of her butt. It was seventh heaven as she embraced me in 69. Her hands roamed over my legs as I pulled her pussy down and extended my tongue into the soft tissue. I felt a tremor run through her body and she choked my member harder. She slowly drew off and extricated herself from my tongue and hands which she had to peel away.

"Good morning," she cooed stroking my face, "Did you dream well?"

"Waking up to you always makes me dream well," I gazed into those softly burning blue eyes. Then something unexpected happened, she broke form. I mean we'd had sex before but this time she broke down. She dived on top of me and rode me like an animal for what felt like days. She ordered me about and I made every effort to do as she said. My penis was deep inside this Goddess and she was fierce this morning. I stroked her blonde hair and kissed her moist full lips.

"Tell me you love me!"

"What?"

"I want to hear the words," she stroked my face as my penis rose and fell to the work of her hips. I choked back, "Say it!"

"I love you," she held me close and kissed softly and tenderly and then she cried. This was most irregular. We'd been told that love was universal. Of course we loved each other, we all did but to have a special attachment to anyone but the Goddess (our sensei) was strictly forbidden. It felt weird to say it anyway. There was nothing special between Starflower and myself. I'd never found her to be anything but a great controlling ride and now …

"I'm sorry," she said between tears. I rubbed the tears off her face.

"It's Ok,"

She stood up and suddenly stopped crying, "Don't tell the Goddess!" she pointed at me, leaving me aching for more.

"Of course not,"

She smiled at me, wiped her eyes and left me to relieve myself before breakfast.

This was all very confusing. Starflower sat next to me at breakfast as usual and worked my leg whilst the Goddess talked to us about the healthy absence of anything artificial including media. Kammil would have approved. There was no sign that anything was wrong with Starflower – and maybe there wasn't.

It was after breakfast. Balls and I had been working in the field, pulling weeds and cutting rice as was usually our trade, when the Goddess, Amber and Starflower all emerged together. They had dressed up in all their finery and the three of them looked electrifying. The Goddess had the sapphire in the middle of her forehead so I knew something good was about to happen. Aba, Gambino and Ualtar were behind them. I looked to Starflower whose face was super cool with a fake smile. I knew her that well at least.

"Balls," the Goddess cooed, "and Marc, come here," I really needed a cool nickname – or maybe a cool drink. Less Coolade anyway. We put our tools down and went over to where the Goddess beckoned us, "We've decided we're going to have a concert," Balls practically leaped up and down with joy.

"A concert?" I asked smiling.

"There is no instrument like the human voice," the Goddess' luminous, green eyes turned to me. I had to agree with her. It wasn't just the presence of her deep eyes. An … undefined period with the Sisterhood really had convinced me that there was no instrument like the human voice.

"There are sounds that only the human animal can make," Amber purred.

"And subtleties that only a human can produce," Starflower added.

"Like birds singing in the trees," the Goddess's voice swayed and I swayed with her, "The heavenly voice of natural sounds,"

The three servants were smiling, eyes glowing with joy as they sat on the grass behind us.

"Balls," the Goddess' eyes swung from me. Balls leapt in the air, "Yes Goddess!" he cried. "Come here," Daniel Balls went over to her, "Kneel," he knelt. I watched feeling a little hesitant.

"Remove your shirt," the Goddess commanded.

Daniel began removing his shirt, "Don't worry Marc," he must have seen my face, "This is *perfect*,"

"Now your belt," Balls did as he was told. Quite a good body for a 50-year-old.

"Good work Balls," Amber cooed.

"Pants," said Starflower as she looked at me and I'd never felt so aroused. Or was that a glint of sorrow in Starflower's eyes?

I felt jealous of Balls as he stripped, in nature, before these 3 Goddesses. He looked so powerless as he knelt before them, naked, like in some Pagan festival, clothes strewn about him. He looked up at them with waiting child's eyes.

The Goddess knelt next to him, "Turn around," her eyes pierced him and Balls turned around so his back was to her. Her arms came around him and he started to moan.

"Balls has been with us for *longer* than you Marc," she breathed into Balls' ear, "so he's very *sensitive* to nature" Ball's head went back as the Goddess ground her hand into Ball's balding hair, "Almost no toxins and a very clear head,". I stood there with a massive hard on and Amber and Starflower grinning at me.

"See if you can pick out this tune Marc,"

Then she began to play. Her hands worked Daniel slowly as her lips, hips and arms worked him. His voice began to slide up and down notes as suddenly soft ahhs became strong ahhs. She stopped for a second and Ball's panted as she held him, "That's just the warm up and tuning," she whispered into Ball's ear. Then she began working him with her hands. She slid over him relentlessly, up and down his naked body with all of us watching. Me with a massive hard on and feeling so jealous and frightened. Balls began to cry and he was crying out a tune I knew! The Goddess' expert arms and lips on Balls and he shuddered out the tune. How could I miss it, it was 'Tchaikovsky's Piano Concerto Number 1'! How was she doing this? After what felt like years watching this humiliated man she gently let go, "Good work Balls," and she kissed his head.

Balls slowly collapsed to the ground, panting, grinning and sighing with pleasure.

The Goddess stood and suddenly her eyes enveloped me. I had practically come watching this performance. She could make music with her members! It was a perfect rendition. What would she do with me? "You see Marc. With a certain free spirit and my expert control we can make beautiful music together," I swallowed and wanted to make beautiful music with her, "You've been with us for a while Marc. You're a sensitive and natural man now. I think we can make music together. Rise Balls," Amber and Starflower helped Balls get up and he went and sat with the three servants.

With her fingers and that all embracing grin the Goddess beckoned me over. I walked over as if in a trance. I started undressing.

"Slow down Marc," ordered Amber.

"Shirt," the Goddess said into my ear as she pushed me down to my knees. I slowly stripped my shirt.

"Trousers," the Goddess said somehow impossibly close to my ear. Soon I was naked, knelt on the ground with the fiercest member facing the Goddess and the Amazon.

"Turn around now Marc," the Goddess breathed into my ear, "Let my hands and lips lead and you'll find your perfect voice," A heavenly hand stroked my back and the top of my head. Her lips touched on the back of my neck and then it began. I resisted for what felt like a second but her expert hands and lips, soon the voice was breaking out of me and the music! Her lips and hands were exquisite. The utter surrender of my body to her warm hands and expert lips and then from somewhere I began to recognised the sounds coming out of me. It was 'Flight of the Bumblebee'. I'd never heard such a perfect rendition than with my own ecstatic voice. The Goddess finally finished swirling her hands around my now super sensitive body. She kissed my ear and gently blew into it, "Well done boy,". I collapsed into a puddle of utterly seduced, exhausted and controlled joy.

I heard applause from somewhere. I twitched on the ground in humiliated, controlled, rubbed to heavenly joy. Balls helped me up.

"You are both great instruments of pure joy now," the Goddess informed us as we stood before her naked, "And you'll find that your singing will get more and more natural as time goes by. Take time to relax now. You've done well," she patted us on the shoulder. Amber and Starflower smiled as they all walked back inside. Starflower looked back at me. Balls smiled at me and me at him as I shuddered with shaking hands to put my clothes back on. Another perfect day with the Sisterhood, another perfect day with the Goddess.

I saw an anaconda. The giant snake came to us and slowly made its way around my building. It was evening and it sunned itself on my back porch. I wanted to have my roughly weekly smoke (actually I smoked whenever I felt like it, which was almost never – but tonight was different) but I couldn't leave my tiny hut. The anaconda looked so regal laying there and wasn't afraid of Balls or myself as we stared. I thought about the Moura Encantada and the terrifying snake that she could turn into. Was this heaven? Was this real? Was this nature? Certainly it was more natural than the world I'd come from – but what could be more natural than one man ruling over another? I felt stupid but – had I just traded in one oligarch for a matriarch. Admittedly oligarchs you never get to meet and I could actually *be* with this matriarch and she was the greatest leader my life had ever known. I was increasing in wisdom and she was right, it is all about nature. No oversized billboards and models looking down on us. No crass commercial TV and no fear mongering news. No processed foods robbing us of subtle tastes, flavours and nutrients. No toxins in my body or mind and people who spent time talking to people not constantly plugged into an unreal world of their phones. I felt like I'd finally woken up and every single moment was a miracle. So why did I feel so uneasy? Was it the way the Goddess had played me like an instrument (the way we'd been played our entire lives - so we were told), I mean I had enjoyed it. I made some beautiful music with her (in many ways) and it was bliss, humiliating and degradingly wonderful. All of which I loved. So why? Was it Starflower who looked at me when the Goddess wasn't around? Was she unloved? We all felt loved here. And we were, weren't we? Was that little performance to humiliate Starflower and cement our loyalty? Maybe. Either way I resolved that I'd learnt all that I could from this leader (she was no Goddess really) and it was time for me to return to the "real" world. Did I really want that? 40 hours a week (which were really 60 when all's told) and commercial nonsense rattling around trying to control my consciousness. Still I could beat it now so I could live free as I chose. I resolved to do that. Do what I came here to do and ask the Goddess for my freedom.

I was in her boudoir. The Goddess had seduced me, drugged me and all ten of her magnificent arms were worshipping me. I was naked and held as indeed I held the Goddess. Our kisses were deep and I succumbed deeper with each and every one. I slid into the Goddess and every inch of me entered a deeper, more silken heaven. Her eyes held me and she smiled through the smoke and steady, relaxing drum beats. I was off in the universe of erotic, all senses deep in heaven. And it was through that smoky haze, into those beaming and powerful, deep green eyes that I spoke and I asked.

"Oh Goddess, you are so merciful and so kind,"

"I am?"

"Yes you are. And I've learnt so much from my time with you and the Sisterhood,"

"There's still a long way to go Marc," she pushed me down, I kissed my way down her and her thighs came over my shoulders locking me gently in place. I looked up at her with my head held gently in position.

"… I feel that I've learnt all that I can from being here … I want to return to the world I knew,"

"Why?" her eyes searched me and I asked myself why.

"Because … I need to be free,"

The Goddess laughed, "This the freedom you sought Marc,"

"You and Amber and Starflower are amazing. As is everyone in the Sisterhood," I struggled to keep my head up in the drug induced haze. I wanted to dive my tongue into that silken pussy. Squeezed between two perfect thighs.

"Mmmmm,"

"It's just I have my own life,"

"Did you have your own life? Is this a life?"

"It is a life, an amazing life and I've seen and grown so much. I love it!" the Goddess squeezed subtly tighter.

"So why leave?" the Goddess stroked my face as another hand pulled slowly on my member. My head went back, "Because ..."

"Yesss,"

"Because ... I have to live by my own rules,"

"You want thisss," the Goddess blew on my ear.

"I do!"

"So you want to stay," she blew and her hand squeezed tighter below.

"In a ... way ... but,"

"Mmmmmm,"

"Let me go. Goddess please,"

Head squeezed, member held, I trembled as I looked into those warm and deep green eyes. And then she said ...

"I'm sorry Marc, NO," ... It took me a second and then it hit me like a blow to the back of the head. I was suddenly shocked 3 quarters awake. Funnily enough all her arms remained. "What do you mean no?"

"I mean you still have far to go and a lot to learn. If you left now you'd regret it forever," she stroked my face.

"I want to go!"

"I'm sorry Marc, NO!" Her words hit me with such force that I woke up. It was cold. I almost wanted to obey and let those blissful arms take me … but I didn't. Instead I struggled against her thighs which were too powerful.

"Marc you really don't want to leave. It's all control out there and the illusion of freedom. You're free here," she cooed, thighs moving and stroking my face. I shuddered and kissed her immaculate thigh.

"Let yourself sink in Marc,"

Suddenly I was pushing against her thighs again and two of her arms gently peeled me off.

"Resist a perfect world with a perfect Goddess, it makes no sense Marc, none of this makes any sense. Return to the core of me," a thigh stroked love into my face.

I couldn't resist under all those arms, thighs and that voice, "No!" I said from somewhere. Then I bit her thigh hard.

She yelled and suddenly I was standing up, panting and sweating.

The Goddess glared at me as I stumbled over to my clothes laying on the floor and proceeded to pull out a smoke and the lighter.

"You're not thinking clearly Marc. You want to leave a world of bliss for hell," the Goddess stood up.

"Your world is amazing and I love it," I said as I pulled out my lighter and I began to unscrew it, "But ..."

"Yesss," the Goddess opened her arms, stroked herself with two and those green eyes made me stumble as I said, "I want to go home,"

The Goddess rose with arms spread, "This is your home Marc," I started to panic, I couldn't let her touch me again. I pulled the lighter apart faster and reassembled it as the Goddess slowly advanced on me, "And are you presuming to smoke in front of me Marc?" green eyes pushing their way through me, "Relax boy," a heavenly hand stroked my hair, "You've got all you need," those smiling eyes enveloped me.

"Dear Goddess," I shook myself awake, "I would never presume to smoke in front of you. Hands up. All of them," and I was aiming a tiny golden gun at her - I know, I'm not original.

The Goddess stared at the weapon I'd just made, "That isn't loaded," the sexiness in her voice was gone.

"I'm afraid it is. One shot. This is a derringer. Probably something you've never heard of, so I'll explain. It's a one-shot pistol for getting out of extremely sticky situations,"

"What's the calibre?"

"Does it matter? Tiny, but if I fire it at this range you may die. Were a long way from medical help Goddess,"

"Amber is a qualified doctor," The Goddess said with her arms covering herself. All except two that stayed in front of me.

"Of course she is. Then I won't feel so guilty for shooting you. Get dressed!"

The Goddess began pulling on her clothes. I really would miss those sumptuous breasts … and the rest of her.

"First you're going to open the safe and I'm going to get my gun,"

"It's not there," she cooed.

"You expect me to believe that! Second, you're going to write a letter and sign it for me to take to the Sisterhood, releasing me from their contracts,"

"You're still contracted to me Marc," the Goddess smiled.

"No I'm not," I said firmly, "now move!"

She wasn't lying, the gun was gone. I was looking into the empty safe, behind the end of the world painting, in the Goddess' office. My personal effects were in there (which I took) but the Gloc was gone. I breathed slowly to steady my panicking nerves.

"Where did you get the guns anyway Marc?"

"Let's simply say that E-bay has an extremely long reach,"

The Goddess moved towards the stairs. "That's far enough!" I thought the Goddess would run off.

"Amber!" the Goddess called downstairs.

"Yes Goddess?"

"Tell Gambino to fire up the generator and Ualtar to align the satellite dish,"

"... Is everything ok?"

"Everything is fine. We just have need to contact the outside world," The Goddess walked back towards me but I stood my ground, "Do you mind?" she asked and I got out of her way. I kept the gun trained on her as she opened a cabinet under the desk. There was a laptop computer in there! She took out the laptop and attached a cable from the wall.

"A computer hey? Nice to avoid anything unnatural,"

"Sometimes we have need of technology," then I heard the generator fire up in the back yard. I looked out the window and saw Gambino with a large portable generator. Black smoke began belching into the air.

"Like now," the Goddess powered up the computer and I never knew how much I missed the hum of little fans and servos powering up.

Someone was coming up the stairs. "Send them away," I whispered.

"Wait!" the Goddess called.

"Are you ok?" Starflower asked.

"Everything is fine. Go back downstairs and tell the slaves to stay in their house," I pressed the gun into her back.

"Ok my Goddess," I heard her steps fade away.

"Slaves eh? Nice to see you believe in personal freedoms,"

"Those three will tear you apart if they catch you with a gun on me," The Goddess ignored me and opened the internet. "What are you doing?" I asked remembering that I was supposed to be in charge.

"Sending an e-mail. You're demanding freedom aren't you?"

I waited as the Goddess connected to Adelene in Paris and I watched her type the words that I'd both longed for and dreaded. 'I hereby grant Marc Durwood freedom from the Sisterhood. He is to be left alone by all members, signed Goddess,'

"Send," I ordered and the Goddess hit the button. I thought of Amanda and my heart ripped in two. All the amazing experiences I'd had. It was over. I was free, if I could get home. I thought about what was waiting for me downstairs and beyond.

"Now come with me," I ordered the Goddess.

I kept the Goddess close as we walked down those stairs.

We emerged to find Starflower, Amber and Balls waiting for us. Balls had my Gloc. I pressed the Derringer into the Goddess' back.

"Steady Marc," Balls began, "nobody wants to hurt anybody,"

"So don't make me. Gun on the floor Balls," he hesitated, "Now!"

"I won't make any sudden moves," Balls gently placed the Gloc on the floor but very close to himself. I'd have to step into the three to get it.

"Kick the gun to me,"

Balls kicked the Gloc, but away under a cabinet, "Not a chance," he said.

I backed the Goddess and myself towards the back door as they shuffled around us. "Was that a good move Balls?" I looked Starflower in her eyes, "Sorry everyone. Don't follow me Balls," I ordered with my back to the door, "Stay inside all of you. When I get to the river I'll release your Goddess,"

"Ok," said Amber, "We won't follow you,"

I smiled one last time at Starflower as I backed the Goddess into the garden.

"Marc think about what you're heading back to. Don't you ever think about how 1% control 99%? Do you think it's natural?" the sexiness in her voice was long gone.

"Shut up!"

"Think about it Marc. They've been in your head since you were 2 years old! You think they'll let you go!?"

"Yeah but now you've set me free now. I can choose!" I pushed the Goddess up the path through the rice field.

"You don't get away that easily. They've made the world so depressing that a quarter of the population needs anti-depressants just to get by. To say nothing of the drug addicts. Marc this is who you really are,"

"I KNOW VERY WELL WHO I AM!"

She stopped talking and we reached the end of the rice field. I looked into the jungle and all the natural noises beyond.

"You won't last *long* out there Marc,"

"Oh please are you still trying it?!"

"Running on a treadmill for the oligarchs Marc, going nowhere," she drew circles in the air, "you are loved, you are cared for, watch TV, eat filth, buy shit, you can't change your life,"

"All right, it's true, it's all true! It's all cults, inside cults, inside cults but that doesn't excuse what you do!"

The Goddess turned and ran. It was the last I ever saw of her. I looked after her. Even if I had fired she wouldn't have been hurt and I was never going to anyway. I turned and ran into the Amazon.

I pelted along the path as all the birds, monkeys and I thought enchanted snakes seemed to be mocking me with their cries. I listened for the sound of pursuers and I never knew I had such speed. I think my fitness had increased. I pelted through that long grass. And I wasn't afraid of nature anymore but man, horrible, horrible man. The scariest creature of all. Before I knew it I was at the river and at that tiny piece of civilisation that would take me home - The Goddess' boat. I jumped in, slipped the rope and struggled to fire up the engine. It hadn't been used in over 3 months. It putted into life.

"Hold those balls!"

No! I slowly turned in the boat and saw Balls, my own gun trained on me. We stood there looking at each other. The boat was slowly puttering away but I'm sure Balls couldn't miss at that range, "Are you going to kill me Balls?" I was prepared for a yes. Instead he smiled and lowered the weapon, "Kill an upstanding man like yourself, never! Although I think you're a fool," he smiled.

"Maybe but I'll be a fool in the world,"

"Good luck Marc let's hope we never meet again,"

"Second that … or you could come with me,"

"Are you kidding? I've found my home. I'm the personal bodyguard to a real live Goddess,"

I smiled at him and Balls at me. We heard the three slaves coming up behind us.

"You'd better go," Balls said, "The three have been with her much longer. I don't think they'll be as forgiving as I am," I smiled and cranked the motor to full power. A few moments later I was through the estuary, onto the open Amazon and freedom. And funnily enough I looked back.

I was at a large, old payphone stuck to the side of the tiny general store that was the only store on the one street town that is Anori.

"Zarek?!" I said down the line as he picked up.

"That is me,"

"It's Marc Durwood. I'm free,"

"I doubt that Mr Durwood. Are you in the centre of town?"

"I am,"

"I'll come find you,"

I worried about Aba, Gambino and Ualtar showing up but I needn't have. I'd stolen their boat and unless they had another I had a solid head start. Zarek met me at the pay phone with a small crowd of excited and confused villagers looking on.

"So Mr Durwood, tell me all about the gold and the virgins?"

"Gold ... everywhere and definitely no virgins," he shook my hand in both of his.

"Come Mr Dorwood, we're having feijoada at my place. You look like you need a hearty meal," and we went off to a well-deserved meal.

That night Zarek dropped me back up river to Manaus and I slept peacefully, two inches from the water surrounded by wildlife. A few days later I was in Rio and on a flight back to the US. The land of the free, the home of the brave or something. I'd definitely never felt so free.

When I returned home I discovered that I had been away for over a year. Obviously, I'd slept some of it. Luckily all the bills pay on autopilot, but my funds were next to dry. I caught up on social media but couldn't explain what had happened to me – especially over Facebook. It seems the cult of far-right politics had advanced considerably whilst I was away. Everyone was relieved that I was safe anyway. Now I needed to face my boss Ms Harris at uni and I finally knew what I had to say.

I sat in her plain white office and waited for her to respond. She was quite pretty, even if she was a little dumpy, but those black stockings and crossed legs were setting me off. So I pretended not to notice.

"Yes, I can see why you didn't e-mail it in," she said after a while.

"And every bit of it is true,"

"Are you seeing a psychologist Marc?"

"Do you really think I need one?"

"You seem sensible enough to me, but you might need deprogramming. There are experts in this kind of thing,"

"I'm not sure if I really want to,"

"That's exactly why you need it. The bit that has me most concerned is this bit,"

"Me offering my resignation?"

"Yes Marc … why?"

"… Because I thought about it. I did the wrong thing. It seems like the only right thing to do,"

"That's very sweet Marc that you're considering us and want to play by the book, but would that serve you?"

"Well no,"

"Would that serve anyone else?"

"My students, the university, the law?"

"You broke no laws Marc, only rules. You really want to do this for moral reasons? We wouldn't benefit by losing you and neither would they,"

"I … broke the rules. Sure, there may have been mitigating circumstances, but it was me who's responsible,"

"That's nice,"

"Is that all you have to say?"

"What would you like me to say Marc?"

"How about we'll hang you from the highest yard arm and make an example out of you, that's what!"

"You're sweet Marc clearly you haven't thought this through,"

Her statement left me dumbfounded and wondering if she was in league with the Goddess.

"I mean think about it. The Russian Mafia are running the White House, politicians are cutting my budget, poverty is increasing and sweeping across our streets and life across the world deteriorates every day. All for the sake of a few criminals in power,"

"Cult leaders,"

Ms Harris swallowed, "Exactly. And you're worried about the rules! Marc you're a great lecturer and researcher. And you're willing to throw it all away over a little consensual sex,"

"There wasn't a little, there was a lot,"

"Good for you,"

"But ... if we don't follow the rules Ms Harris isn't it all just meaningless? I mean then it's all just a jungle, like the Amazon,"

"There's the rule of nature and that's life. People doing the best they can with the limited resources they have in, yes, a lawless jungle,"

"What about the law of the cults?"

"But you've decided not to follow the cults,"

"It's all cults! The cult of capitalism, the cult of communism, the cult of oligarchy, America, Australia, Japan, this university – all cults. Everyone is poking around in each other's head and screwing each other over and it's anyone's game,"

"Marc, at least you got to choose the cult you play for. Not many people in the world get that opportunity,"

"Very true,"

"So, I'm staying?"

"I wouldn't have it any other way," and she counter crossed her legs. I looked the other way.

"Oh, one more thing,"

"What's that Marc?"

"I want to teach one subject. 20 hours a week,"

"May I ask why?"

"I ... want to live my life,"

Ms Harris smiled, "Of course you can. You've always got free will Marc," she smiled, "Now get out there and just do the best you can,"

"Thank you Ms Harris," I smiled, left her office and stepped back into the world.

It was a few days later and I was settling back into my office (which amazingly hadn't been taken over). It felt strange but good to be at my home away from home when a knock came at my door.

"Who is it?"

"It's me," Amanda's voice, "May I come in?" I swallowed, straightened my jacket and walked to the door. Heart thumping because of who was waiting on the other side. I opened the door for her. Amanda was in a cream jumper with her radiant blonde bobbing hair, creamy skin, lightly tanned in a short denim skirt and a sheepish expression. She looked at me with upturned eyes.

"Amanda," I smiled at her, "Come on in. Take a seat," I closed the door and Amanda sat on my couch. I took out my comfy office chair and sat across from her.

"Are you Ok?" I asked.

"You're asking if I'm ok. I'm the one who should be asking you,"

"So ask," I smiled.

"Are you Ok?"

"Never better, you?" she really did look amazing with those deep blue, apprehensive eyes.

"I … got a message the other day. We're to leave you alone … We did you wrong,"

"Apparently yes. Tea?"

"No thanks. I won't hold you up long. Oh sorry, I forgot!"

"Amanda, it's ok. I've seen incredible things. A whole world I never knew existed and it's all because of you,"

"Plus Iris and Rachelle,"

"Well they helped yes,"

"You're not angry?" she leaned forward and I got the hint of pale mountains rolling into view. I swallowed.

"I was before but not now. Sure you won't have some tea?"

"No thank you sir,"

"Please don't call me sir," I laughed and looked into her pale, sorrowful eyes.

"Are you leaving us?"

"Actually I'm happy to say I'm staying … Amanda, I've got to say I really like you," Her eyes lit up, "And not just the dominant you and I like that too. But The whole you," I was well out of order now along with the whole cultish country and the whole cultish world. Lawless pyramids, stacked on pyramids – welcome to nature, "I don't think you did any wrong,"

"Really?!"

"Yes and you brought me to a deeper understanding of myself. I think this … thing we have, could be a lot of fun, in moderation. All things in moderation especially moderation. I think we just need some agreement to swim between the flags,"

"You'll … follow me?"

"From time to time yes,"

"Can Iris and Rachelle come too?"

"Sometimes yes," I conceded, "But it's you I want," we looked into each other's eyes.

A knock came at the door, "I'm busy!"

"It's us," Iris' familiar voice called out. I looked at smiling Amanda, "Come in,"

The door opened and in came Rachelle and Iris. They both looked amazing. They walked in slowly and sat down on the couch. Iris sat on the arm of the couch. Rachelle sat next to Amanda. I looked from Rachelle's tanned, toned thighs to her green eyes to Iris in her floral short dress, marble legs and brown eyes, to Amanda in her short skirt and just the tiniest hint of pink panties.

"You two were outside,"

"Not for all of it," said Iris

"You heard what I said?"

"We did," and Rachelle stroked her thigh.

I smiled, "Well Amanda, Iris, Rachelle, in that case," I looked around into their deep, beautiful eyes, "What can I do for you?"

THE END

Thanks for reading. If you enjoyed this then please try my other works from the compiled book Unstoppable or read individually ...

Stand Alone Books

Shrink: Lydia the Sexy Psychologist

Trumped: How the President became my Slave

Meagan: My Daughter's Friend

Alysha: Moved In

Sexpocalypse: My Greatest Wish

The Sisterhood Series

The Terrible 3: I Mean Terrific 3

Running From / Towards the Sisterhood

When in Paris and Borneo

The Goddess

Like the Story? Please review it on Amazon.com

Your opinion makes a big difference to other readers and myself.

Follow the conversation on my blog. We're about to go into interesting territory. Also available at my Amazon Author Page.

E-mail me at michaelwhiteerotica@gmail.com

Thanks again and enjoy!!

Made in the USA
San Bernardino, CA
28 December 2019